Please return this book on or before the date shown above. To renew go to www.essex.gov.uk/libraries, ring 0845 603 7628 or go to any Essex library.

LOUGHTON

Essex County Council

KEEPING SECRETS

Twenty-two years ago, Joanna gave up her baby girl for adoption, but she has never forgotten her. When Caroline comes back into her life Joanna is both thrilled and afraid: her son, Robbie, doesn't know about Caroline's existence, and Joanna's marriage to Mike is in crisis. Her long lost daughter couldn't have arrived at a more turbulent moment. Only time will tell if Caroline's presence will reunite the family or destroy it altogether . . .

DELLA GALTON

KEEPING
SECRETS

Complete and Unabridged

LINFORD
Leicester

First published in Great Britain in 2002

First Linford Edition
published 2012

British Library CIP Data

Galton, Della.
    Keeping secrets. - - (Linford romance library)
    1. Love stories.
    2. Large type books.
    I. Title II. Series
    823.9'2–dc23

    ISBN 978–1–4448–1252–7

Published by
F. A. Thorpe (Publishing)
Anstey, Leicestershire

Set by Words & Graphics Ltd.
Anstey, Leicestershire
Printed and bound in Great Britain by
T. J. International Ltd., Padstow, Cornwall

This book is printed on acid-free paper

1

I'd dreamed about this moment for more than half my life, thought I'd prepared myself for it — well, as much as you ever could. But now it had happened, I realised that I wasn't prepared at all. The first thump of shock had turned into a strange mixture of emotions: delight, terror and exhilaration.

I stood on the landing, gazing out of the big bay window that overlooked the pier. Beyond the pier, the sea stretched flat and grey beneath the November sky. Then my eyes were drawn back to Ian Sanderson's car, which was just pulling up the hill on to the coast road, exhaust fumes chugging from it. He couldn't make much money out of delivering bombshells, I thought.

I hadn't suspected anything when I'd opened the door. I'd thought he was just another late tourist, drawn by the 'vacancies' sign in the window. He'd looked presentable enough. I guessed him to be fortyish, same age as me. He had dark hair and was clean-shaven, his clothes well-worn but neat. I prided myself on being able to sum up doorstep callers in an instant. Judge whether they were likely to be trouble or not. That was important these days, now Mike was no longer around.

'Good afternoon,' he'd said pleasantly. 'Is it possible to speak to Joanna Cartwright?'

'You're speaking to her,' I said, equally pleasantly. 'How can I help?'

'Ian Sanderson.' He held out a card. 'I'm from a company called Reunited.'

I nodded, not really paying attention. I was about to launch into my 'no thank you' speech when he said, 'I'm here on behalf of Caroline Patterson.'

That was when I felt the first little thump of shock. Patterson had been my maiden name and Caroline the name of the baby girl I'd given up for adoption twenty-two years earlier.

For a moment we just stared at each other and if he noticed I was clutching the front door harder than I'd been a moment before, he gave no sign of it. He just stood there, patiently waiting for me to absorb what he'd said.

'You'd better come in,' I said at last, and he nodded, dropping his gaze momentarily as if he was used to this. Which I suppose, with hindsight, he was.

I led him along the hallway, through our tiny reception area into the kitchen. I'd just finished cleaning the plates from the few breakfasts I'd done that morning. It was a week until the end of the season and apart from Mabel and George, an elderly couple who came every year, the hotel was empty. In the kitchen I gestured for him to sit on a stool at the central breakfast bar, then filled up the kettle, needing some time just to collect myself before he said whatever it was he'd come to say. Cold water splashed over my hands into the huge industrial sink, but eventually I got the kettle half-full and plugged it in. Then I took a deep breath and turned round to face him.

'I realise this must be a shock, Mrs Cartwright,' he began quietly.

I nodded and sat opposite him, keeping my hands in my lap where he wouldn't see them and guess just how much of a shock it was.

'My company traces people. For all sorts of reasons, but we specialise in adoption cases.' He glanced at me, as if trying to gauge my reaction. 'If this isn't a good time, I could come back. Some time more convenient?'

'Now's fine,' I said, wondering how often people took him up on that. Told him it would never be convenient for him to disrupt their lives, to bring out their long-forgotten skeletons.

He produced some paperwork from a file he was carrying. 'Caroline contacted us three weeks ago and asked us to trace you.'

It hadn't taken them long, I thought, to unravel the years. Pictures of the last three weeks flashed into my head and for a moment I wondered how it was that I hadn't sensed my daughter's intentions, picked up something from the ether. But then so much had happened recently. Robbie, my son and Caroline's brother, had moved out for the first time. Her father and I had decided to sell the hotel and get a divorce. Caroline couldn't have picked a more turbulent time in my life if she'd tried.

'She wants to meet you,' Ian continued. 'She's asked us to act as intermediaries because she didn't just want to turn up out of the blue, bearing in mind that you were married and might well have another family who knew nothing of her existence. She didn't want to put you in a difficult position.'

'I see,' I said, but all I could think about was that she wanted to meet me. My little girl didn't hate me. She couldn't, if she wanted to meet me, if she'd gone to all this trouble to track me down.

'My job was to find you and ask

how you'd feel about seeing her,' Ian continued. 'And then to pass on your answer, either way.' He paused and looked at me.

'Do a lot of people say no?' I couldn't believe how calm my voice sounded.

'Some do. It depends on what the circumstances are now. For some people the past is so painful they just want to forget it.'

I nodded. I could understand that. I'd spent a lot of time trying to forget, although I don't think I'd ever really managed it. I'd buried my feelings, but it had always been temporary. They'd always surfaced again. Sometimes in nightmares, sometimes in guilt, sometimes in a vague restlessness I couldn't put my finger on.

Now there was a part of me that wanted to throw my arms around Ian Sanderson and say, 'What are you waiting for? Go and get her now!' But I didn't, of course. I just met his eyes and said steadily, 'I've always hoped she'd get in touch.'

That was the understatement of the century, but it was as much as he was going to get. I had no intention of pouring out my heart to him. Besides, I'd got pretty good at concealing my feelings these last few weeks.

Behind me, the kettle clicked off. 'Would you like a coffee?'

'Thank you.'

I took my time over making it. It was easier to talk to him with my back turned. 'So is she all right? Where's she living now? What's she doing?' The words sounded inane, but it was hard to know where to start. Somehow I'd always expected that if this moment ever came, it would be Caroline I'd be talking to, not some stranger she'd sent in her place to check out the lie of the land.

'She's fine,' he said. 'She's working and she's happy. I'm sorry I can't tell you her address. She has to tell you that herself. But she's not a million miles from here.'

I put a mug of coffee in front of him and he thanked me.

7

'I bet you get some mixed reactions, don't you?'

'Yes.' The faintest of smiles warmed his dark eyes, but he didn't elaborate.

'Well, you can tell her I'd be happy to meet her. How does it work? Will you just pass on my address?'

'I can ask her to phone you first, if you like?'

'Yes, that would be better. Then we could arrange a good time.' Who was I trying to kid? I wanted her to phone first, so I'd have time to psyche myself up, prepare — if that were possible.

Ian Sanderson finished his coffee before I was halfway through mine. 'I'll tell her what you've said, Mrs Cartwright.' He got up. 'Thanks. If there's anything else you want to ask me, here's my card.'

I took it, knowing I wouldn't use it. Then I went with him back to the front door. The whole visit had taken less than fifteen minutes. A quarter of an hour to stir up twenty-two-year-old memories, I thought, as I closed the front door quietly behind him.

When he'd gone, I went upstairs and watched him get in his car and drive away from the hotel. A part of me was still not convinced it had happened. I couldn't think straight. All I could think about was that I was going to meet Caroline. There was to be no more speculation about what she looked like, how she felt about me. Soon I would know. I'd always wanted to know, but what if I didn't live up to her expectations? My emotions swung wildly between joy and terror. What if she *did* hate me for giving her away?

The doorbell rang again. I glanced out of the window and saw Gail's car on the forecourt. Gail was my oldest and dearest friend and I'd forgotten she'd said she was coming round today. Since Mike had moved out, Gail had taken to calling round a couple of times a week. She was worried about me, she said, although I'd told her she didn't need to be. Mike and I had been on the rocks for so long, it was a relief that he'd finally gone. As well as being my closest friend, I reflected, Gail was also one of the few people in my life who knew about Caroline. What on earth was she going to say about what had just happened? I took a deep breath and went downstairs to let her in.

'Brrr, it's freezing out there. Winter's definitely on the way.' As she spoke, she unbuttoned her coat, put her keys in her pocket and carefully removed her scarf from immaculate blonde hair. Gail never did less than three things at once. 'Got the kettle on?'

She breezed through to the kitchen and I followed behind her, feeling completely numb.

'How's it going?' She looked at me for the first time. 'Hey, Jo, are you all right? You've not had another call from Mike?' She frowned, her blue eyes worried. 'He hasn't changed his mind about the divorce, has he?'

I shook my head, watching her sit on the stool that Ian Sanderson had vacated a short while earlier.

She rested her elbows on the breakfast bar, put her chin in her hands and studied me. 'So what is it, then?'

'You're never going to believe it.'

'Try me.'

'Caroline has tracked me down.' I watched Gail's expression change from puzzlement to dawning realisation to consternation.

'You don't mean your daughter?' she said. 'You mean she's been here? Today?'

'No, not exactly. Not personally. A man came from a tracing agency. You can do that these days — send someone ahead of you to check out the lie of the land. Make sure you're not just blundering in.' I was aware that I was blabbering and that Gail's look of consternation was spreading.

'Slow down and start from the beginning,' she said.

So I did. I told her all about Ian Sanderson's visit and about how I'd been feeling ever since he'd gone, although it was hard to describe that

11

bit. How could you possibly feel delight, terror and exhilaration all at once?

Gail didn't interrupt. She just refilled my mug with tea from time to time and nodded in all the right places. When I finally ground to a halt and started apologising for going on, she said, 'Don't be daft. It's hardly surprising in the circumstances.' She reached for my hands. 'Wow, what a shock.'

'It is, but it's a brilliant shock.' I grinned at her and she squeezed my fingers.

'Are you going to tell Mike?'

'I don't know. I suppose I'll have to. It's Robbie I'm worried about. He doesn't even know he's got a sister. How's he going to cope with knowing we've kept a secret like that from him all these years?'

'It might give him some insight into why you and his father split up,' Gail said quietly.

I looked at her sharply. 'We didn't split up because of Caroline. We both thought the adoption was the right thing to do at the time.'

'I'm not saying you didn't agree about the adoption.' Her voice was soft. 'I'm talking about keeping it a secret from Robbie. Secrets in families are only OK if you both agree that there's a good reason for keeping them.'

I didn't say anything. Gail and I went back so long that it was impossible to hide things from her. I knew — we both knew — that she did have a point.

I'd been just eighteen when I'd fallen pregnant. Mike and I had only been seeing each other for a couple of months and Mike wasn't ready to be a father.

'I've got so many plans, Jo,' he had said. 'We can't have a baby. Not yet.'

'We *are* having one,' I'd whispered. 'What am I supposed to do? Don't ask me to get rid of it.'

'I wouldn't do that.' Mike looked shocked. 'But there are other options. Loads of couples are desperate to have children and can't. Think about them,

Jo. Think about what's best for the baby. We have to be unselfish about this.'

'You mean I should think about having our baby adopted?' I'd said bleakly.

'It might be for the best, sweetheart,' he told me. 'We're not ready for that sort of responsibility. We've no money, no home. Think about it rationally.'

I'd stared into his blue eyes and thought yes, he's right. Adoption would be a good option. Not because I agreed with him that we had nothing to offer, but because I knew he wasn't ready to be a father. I had this crazy, idealistic notion that a baby needed both parents to be fully committed.

So we'd gone ahead and had Caroline adopted. Mike had seemed happy and I'd never told him about the nightmares I'd had for weeks after her birth. The nightmares about the baby in the cupboard the locked away baby I hadn't been allowed to look after, or even see for very long. I'd never told Mike about the increasing longing I'd felt as the years went by and I didn't know what my little girl looked like as she grew up. Even Robbie's birth three years later hadn't done much to alleviate the sense of loss.

'I want to show you something, Gail,' I said suddenly.

'What?'

'Just come upstairs a minute.'

She must have heard the urgency in my voice because she stared at me for a second and said, 'Of course.' As we walked upstairs, she said, 'How's everything going with the sale?'

'Slowly. The estate agent reckons we'll get more if we can sell the hotel as development land. Every other hotel between here and the pier's already been converted into flats.'

'So will you?'

'Yes, if we can. To be honest, Gail, I don't really care any more. I just want out.'

As we reached the first landing, she touched my arm. 'Yes, I'm not surprised,' she said.

I took her up the next flight of stairs to the little box room, which Mike and I hardly ever went in. It was used to store spare mattresses and a couple of ancient cots that we sometimes had to call into service if we had an above average number of babies staying. That was ironic, I thought now, as I pulled the cots out of the way and got down a suitcase that was tucked on the top shelf.

Gail looked at me quizzically but I didn't explain, just dragged the suitcase out onto the landing and swept a fine coating of dust off the brown leather lid. I knelt on the carpet in front of it and Gail sat beside me.

'I've never shown anyone this,' I murmured.

She bit her lip as I flipped up the catches and reached into the case. I took out the outfits one by one. They were all still on their hangers and I hung them round the banisters of the stairs in the same order in which I'd taken them from the case. There was an ivory silk shirt and matching skirt. A linen trouser suit. A pair of faded jeans and denim waistcoat. Moving downwards through the years there was a party dress for an eight-year-old, all lace and little bows. A pair of pale blue dungarees. A tiny red dress, sewn with yellow and blue butterflies, and finally a pink romper suit, for age up to six months. An outfit for every year of Caroline's life and, although I'd known she'd never wear them, each outfit was the very best I could afford. Mike would never let me talk about our daughter, and they were the only way I'd had of keeping her alive.

Gail didn't say anything as I reached one more time into the case and took out a little plastic bag. In it were twenty-one birthday cards. All unopened, but I wrote the same each time. *To Caroline, Happy Birthday, lots of love, Mummy.* In later years, I'd thought that maybe I should have put Mum, but I never had. Caroline would never see these cards. Never even know about them.

'Do you think I'm mad?' I whispered to Gail.

'No, love.' She reached for my hand and there were tears in her eyes. We sat there for a long time in the dim light of the landing, without speaking.

Gail stayed until lunch-time but even though we talked and talked, or rather I burbled on and she did her best to offer advice, by the time she'd left I still wasn't sure what to do for the best. I'd have to phone Mike and tell him what had happened. I knew that. Then between us we could decide how we were going to tell Robbie, because we'd have to tell him now. That was another certainty. Telling Robbie had always been a bone of contention between Mike and me. I'd wanted to tell him years ago, but Mike had said no.

'There's no need, sweetheart,' he'd said, when Robbie was young. 'He won't understand. It will only stir up trouble.' Then later, when I'd pressed him again, he'd just got irritable and changed the subject. Mike hated confrontations of any kind.

I tried to imagine how Robbie would feel. Despite the fact that he'd just moved out into a flat with some college friends, he was a very young eighteen-year-old. He reminded me a bit of how his dad had been at that age: naïve and passionate, in a black-and-white kind of way. There were no shades of grey in Robbie's world. Youth and black-and-white went together, I thought. Grey came later, with maturity. I wondered what would have happened if Caroline hadn't been so considerate about getting in touch with us, if she'd decided to just turn up on our doorstep herself without using the cushion of Ian Sanderson. What would have happened if she'd come round in the last three weeks, rung the doorbell and come face to face with Mike, or with Robbie?

It couldn't really have been any worse, I thought, as I washed the kitchen floor that evening and got the breakfast stuff ready for the next day. Robbie already blamed me for the fact that his father and I were divorcing. We'd had a row the night before he'd moved out. Mike had been sorting out some customer bills in reception, while Robbie helped me put away plates in the kitchen — a sure sign that I was about to get a lecture.

'Dad would try again if you'd let him, you know.'

'This isn't a decision I've made on my own, Robbie,' I told him gently. 'We both feel it's time to go our separate ways.'

'Dad doesn't.' He'd glared at me, his blue eyes, so like Mike's, snapping with fire. 'He'd have you back straight away.'

'It isn't as simple as that, Robbie. Please don't interfere.' I'd glanced up at my son with a mixture of pride and irritation and wondered how it was that I hadn't noticed him getting so tall.

He didn't say anything else, but the way he crashed plates into the cupboard had left me in no doubt as to how he felt and whose fault he thought it was that his father and I were splitting up. I'd bitten my lip and not said anything, as I'd done so many times across the years. Robbie and Mike had always been close. It was one of those bittersweet ironies of life that, although Mike hadn't wanted to be a father, as far as Robbie was concerned he was the greatest dad on the planet.

But then Mike had always been good at the fun bits of fatherhood, I found myself thinking bitterly. Across the years, Mike had loved playing football and building sandcastles on the beach. He'd left all the nasty, responsible, disciplinary bits to me, sliding into the background if there was anything remotely confrontational on the parent-hood agenda. I'd resented him for that. But not as much as I'd resented him for making me keep Caroline a secret.

'We ought to tell Robbie he has a sister,' I'd said to Mike the same evening that Robbie had crashed plates around the kitchen. 'He has a right to know and I think we should tell him while you're still here.'

'What, and give the lad another huge shock? Don't be ridiculous,' Mike snapped, and for once I'd thought he was probably right. This wasn't the best time for confessions.

I'd looked at Mike then. At the tired, familiar face I'd grown up with, the grey streaks in his once jet-black hair, and wondered if it was true what our son had said. If, given the choice, Mike would have wanted us to stay married. He'd agreed readily enough to divorce. It had been on my lips to ask him. To just say quietly, 'Are we doing the right thing, Mike?'

But then he said, 'Don't you think it's about time you accepted the fact that we have one child, Joanna, and that's Robbie? Everything else is in here.' He jabbed a finger at the side of his head and added, 'It's time you let go of the past, isn't it?' His eyes were so cross and cold that the words were swept from my mind.

★ ★ ★

As I laid the dining room for breakfast, I wondered what Mike was going to say when I phoned and told him the past

22

had caught up with us at last.

There was only one elderly couple still in the hotel, Mabel and George, who didn't know yet that this was their last visit. They hadn't noticed that Mike hadn't been around for the last few days either, I thought affectionately. Perhaps that was the key to a long and happy marriage: not noticing things. Just plodding along like a blinkered horse with the security of the harness at your sides, knowing you'll be OK as long as you keep looking straight ahead. Not glancing to your left or right, and certainly never behind you.

I smiled to myself. Now I really was getting fanciful. It was the shock of today's events. Emotions were still swinging at me from all directions. Euphoria was the main one, but I was completely on edge too. Every time the phone rang, I jumped out of my skin. But so far the only calls had been from the fruit and veg man checking I didn't want him to call one last time, and from a couple asking if we were open for

Christmas. Caroline probably wouldn't phone for a few days, I thought. For all I knew, Ian Sanderson hadn't even told her he'd seen me yet. After all, what was it to him? He could have no idea of what it was like to wait for a call you'd feared might never come.

The phone rang again as I was fetching the fruit juice glasses from the kitchen. I pounced on it. 'Sea View Hotel, good evening.'

'Can I speak to Joanna Cartwright, please?' The voice was young, slightly hesitant.

'Speaking,' I said, feeling my heart begin to pound. Because this was her. This was Caroline. I knew it. Every muscle in my body was tense and I was pressing the phone so hard against my ear that it hurt.

'I'm Caroline,' she said. 'Ian told me you wouldn't mind if I called.'

'I don't. I don't mind at all. I mean, I'm really glad you have.' I could hardly breathe.

'I was wondering if perhaps we could

24

meet up,' she said. 'If you're not busy or anything.'

'Of course. I'd love to. When?'

She hesitated, then said, 'I'm in my car at the end of your road. If it's all right with you, I could come down now.'

'Now?' I must have sounded shocked because she said immediately, 'Say if you're busy. I mean, I can come any time.'

'No. Now will be fine,' I said impulsively, because perhaps it was better like this. Better not to have time to tell Ian or Robbie or to prepare myself mentally. Perhaps jumping in the deep end was a good thing to do.

'See you in about five minutes, then,' she said softly, and put the phone down.

I stood there, shaking inside and out. Now? She was coming now and there wasn't even time to put on some make-up and change my clothes and try to look less like the tired, end-of-season hotelier that I was.

Suddenly spurred into action, I ran into the shower room and studied myself in the mirror. I could put my hair up. I always looked better with my hair up. I had huge trouble with the grips because my hands were shaking so much, but I got them in eventually. It didn't make a lot of difference, I thought, studying my reflection. Now I just looked like a tired, end-of-season hotelier with her hair pinned up. I was wearing a black ribbed top, but at least it was clean, and scruffy old leggings with bleach marks on. I was just wrenching them off and pulling on a pair of clean but un-ironed jeans when the doorbell rang.

I sprayed my hair with extra-firm hold hairspray, then took several deep breaths. The doorbell rang again just as I was stepping into the hallway. Goodness, Caroline was impatient! At least I'd have one small advantage, I thought, as I went towards the glass front door. I'd be able to see her, albeit fleetingly, before she saw me. Unless, of course, she was standing with her nose pressed against the glass.

She wasn't, of course. She was standing with her face turned towards the sea, just like any other casual caller, not curious about me at all. If I walked slowly, it would give me the chance for a sneak preview — or at least it would have done if I'd put my glasses on. But as I approached the front door and the person outside came properly into focus, I realised with rapidly increasing panic that it wasn't Caroline who was standing on the doorstep at all. It was Robbie.

2

I opened the door and Robbie grinned at me, but I was too shocked to return his welcome. 'What are you doing here?'

'Well, it's nice to see you too. I thought I'd moved out, not been banished for ever.' He looked irritated, which wasn't surprising, but my heart was pounding so loudly that I could hardly hear myself speak. I had to get rid of him before Caroline turned up.

'Look, Robbie, it's a bit inconvenient at the moment.' I held on to the door so he couldn't get past me.

'What do you mean inconvenient? I only want to pick up some of my stuff.' He looked over my shoulder into the hallway. 'Hey, you haven't got some bloke here, have you? No wonder you were so anxious to kick me and Dad out.'

'Of course I haven't got a bloke here. It's just bad timing. I've got to pop out.'

'At this time of night? What for?'

As he spoke, the headlights of a car drew on to the hotel forecourt. They dimmed as the driver switched off the engine and I could see a young girl in the driver's seat. Caroline. Oh God, this was like some sort of out-of-control soap opera.

Seeing my shocked gaze, Robbie turned and said, 'Well, it looks like you've got a visitor, so you can't go out yet. I'll only be a minute.'

There was nothing to do but let him in. I opened the door wider and he went past me and headed down the hallway. If I was lucky, they wouldn't meet. They couldn't meet now, not like this. Robbie would never forgive me. Neither would Mike, I thought grimly. He wouldn't believe I hadn't engineered it to turn his son against him. Fat chance. It was far more likely that Robbie would hate me for not telling him he had a sister. And what would

Caroline think, finding herself in the middle of a blazing row? It didn't bear thinking about.

I turned my attention back to the girl, who was getting out of the car, rather awkwardly I thought, but it was only when she stood up and slammed the car door that I saw why. My long-lost daughter, if indeed it was Caroline, was heavily pregnant.

A baby, I thought, my senses reeling with a mixture of shock and delight. I stepped forward to meet her. 'Caroline?'

'That's right.' She didn't smile, just gave me a long, cool look. 'You must be Joanna.'

I nodded. She was beautiful, my little girl. She had dark eyes and brown hair, which she wore long and loose, like I'd done at her age. She was pale too, but that was probably the pregnancy. There was a huge ache in my throat and I wanted to hug her. My arms would just about have gone round her, but her face didn't invite it.

'Come in out of the cold,' I said.

'Thanks.' It seemed her eyes softened a bit then, so perhaps I had imagined the coolness. She was probably as nervous as I was. It was hardly an everyday occurrence, meeting your mother for the first time.

'We'll go in the kitchen,' I said. 'It's warm in there. We can talk and I'll make you a nice cup of tea.' Once again, I thought how inadequate words were for a situation like this. I must sound like an idiot. Offering her tea and a warm kitchen as though she were some casual acquaintance, when all I really wanted to do was to hold her in my arms and never let her go again. It was the most curious sensation, looking at my baby all grown up. This child I'd given birth to had become a beautiful woman, yet I knew nothing of all the years between.

'Through here,' I said and, as she went ahead of me along the hallway, I thought she might not even like tea. I prayed that Robbie would stay upstairs until she was in the kitchen. But just as we were going through reception, he put his head over the banisters and called down the stairs.

'Mum, what are all these kiddies' clothes doing up here?' I'd been showing my secret collection to my best friend, Gail, and hadn't got around to putting them away again.

It was too late to stop my son and daughter meeting. She turned her face up towards him and he grinned. This couldn't get any worse, could it? I closed my eyes. When I opened them again, Caroline was studying her brother with open curiosity and Robbie had a speculative look on his face. From that angle, he wouldn't be able to see she was pregnant. All he would see was a pretty face and, with his current hormone level, there was no way he wasn't going to want to investigate further.

'Did you say you were brewing up, Mum? Make one for me. I'll be down in a sec. I've got a message from Dad.'

'Just give us a minute, could you?' To

my amazement my voice sounded normal. Perhaps I could still salvage this. If I could just explain to Caroline that he didn't know about her yet. But as Robbie ignored me and came bounding down the stairs, I knew I wasn't going to get the chance. In a few moments, he'd know he had a sister I'd never thought fit to tell him about. Not to mention the fact there was obviously another relative imminent. Shock had turned not just my legs to jelly but my brain, too. So much for being prepared.

I'd just had time to pull out a stool for Caroline when Robbie appeared in the doorway.

'Who's this, then?' he said, but although the question was aimed at me, he was looking at Caroline. 'I know you can't be a guest because you wouldn't be in the kitchen. It's one of Mum's rules.'

She looked at him, that same appraising look she'd given me, and I held my breath. I'd always hoped they'd meet, but not like this. Then she said softly and without a flicker of discomfort, 'I'm a friend of your mother's.'

There was a microsecond of silence. I glanced at her with what must have looked like pure relief. Robbie, however, was too enchanted to notice. He just went across the kitchen and held out his hand.

'Robbie,' he said politely.

'Caroline.'

'Nice to meet you.'

'You too.' She smiled then and her dark eyes warmed. I felt like a condemned prisoner who's been pardoned at the eleventh hour. Except, of course, that Caroline might change her mind at any moment. There was, after all, no reason on earth why she should protect me. I made tea as fast as my shaking hands would allow.

'I don't want to rush you, but we've got things to talk about,' I told Robbie. 'Girl-type things.' I raised my eyebrows and he grinned, seeming to notice Caroline's condition for the first time.

'Baby talk, is it? Is that why you've

got all my old baby stuff hung round the banisters?'

I didn't say anything. Robbie, typically, had failed to notice they were girl's clothes and therefore nothing to do with him. Not to mention the fact they weren't just baby clothes but went up until well past teenager. My throat ached at the irony of it all. Caroline's face was impassive and I wondered at her calmness. Or perhaps she was as shocked as I was. She hadn't taken her eyes off Robbie since they'd met. Not that I was doing much better. Seeing her and Robbie together was uncanny. They had different coloured eyes, but similar shaped faces and exactly the same nose. Mike's nose.

'Have you got everything then, love?' I said, in an attempt to divert Robbie before he got too comfortable.

'Yeah, for now.' He drained his mug and banged it back down on the side. 'Don't worry. I don't want to get involved in any baby talk. Not for at least another twenty years or so. Sounds too much like hard work to me.'

'I'm looking forward to it,' Caroline said. 'I don't mind hard work.' She didn't so much as glance in my direction, but it seemed to me that an edge of bitterness had crept into her voice — or perhaps my imagination was working overtime again.

I hardly dared to breathe, but Robbie, oblivious to any tension, just grinned and said, 'Well, I guess that's just as well, isn't it? I mean — '

'Robbie,' I interrupted frantically, 'did you say you had a message from Dad?'

'Yes.' He stood up. 'That property developer bloke's coming round in the morning. He says it's best if they meet here. Dad wanted to check it's OK.'

'Of course it's OK. He's got a key, hasn't he?'

'Dad thought he'd better check first.'

'It's fine.' I ushered him out of the kitchen. 'I'll see them both here tomorrow.'

In the hallway he gave me a quick,

suspicious glance. 'Are you regretting it, then? All this?'

'No.'

'You haven't got another fellow have you, Mum? Only you're acting really strangely.'

'Of course I haven't Robbie. Will you just stop it?'

'Dad misses you, you know.'

I glared at him and he frowned and bent to pick up his rucksack. 'Well, I can see it's not mutual. I'll be round later in the week. I'm bound to have forgotten something else.'

'Of course,' I said, and then he was finally out of the door and I felt like collapsing with relief. I hurried back to the kitchen. I was going to get the chance to explain. Get the chance to meet Caroline properly.

She had her back to me. She was standing by the window, which over-looked our back yard, where a string of white sheets from yesterday's depar-tures billowed ghost-like in the dark.

'I'm really sorry,' I said. 'Robbie

arrived unexpectedly, just before you did. I didn't mean for you to meet like that.'

For a few seconds she didn't speak. Then she turned and I could see there were tears rolling down her face. 'I bet you didn't,' she said. Suddenly there was such ice in her voice that I stopped where I was, shocked.

'Caroline?' I took another step forward and she put out her hands, palms facing me.

'Don't. Don't touch me.'

For a few frozen moments neither of us moved. Then she dropped her hands and said in a tight, clipped voice, 'I came to see . . . if I could understand . . . what sort of woman could give up her own child. I thought . . . I thought maybe you'd have regretted it. Maybe even wanted me to get in touch.'

'I did. I've always wanted it. I've always dreamed of it.' My words stumbled over themselves in my haste to explain.

'But I've got a brother and he doesn't

know. And you let me come round.' Her pale face was flushed now, her voice all strange and choked. I ached to go to her. Even as I took another step nearer, protests forming on my lips, she stepped jerkily away from me.

'Don't try and justify yourself. I know how it feels.' She placed both hands over her bump and met my eyes. 'There's nothing on God's earth that would make me give up my baby. Nothing.'

I stared at her, too stunned to react. All the time, inside of me, a tiny, dispassionate voice was saying, 'She's right. You're a coward. What mother would willingly give away her child? She has every right to hate you for it. You deserve this.'

'I didn't want to give you up,' I said at last. 'I just wanted what was best for you.' My words sounded weak and insincere, even to my own ears.

'You wanted to forget me.' Her eyes blazed with the same passion Robbie's had when we'd rowed the previous week. 'You couldn't even tell my brother about me, could you? Did you tell my father? Or did you keep him in the dark, too?'

'That's not fair,' I said, stung, but I could see she wasn't listening. She was breathing very heavily and her face looked whiter than ever. She'd made up her mind about me and nothing I could say was going to change it. She started doing up the coat she'd only partly unbuttoned. Then she spun round and headed out of the kitchen.

'Don't go. Please.' But it was too late. I knew it was too late, even as I chased after her. She hurried along the hallway as fast as her pregnancy would allow. She couldn't wait to get away from me, I realised, something tearing deep inside me. She fumbled with the front door catch and let herself outside. I ran out after her, tears streaming down my face as she got into her car.

'Caroline! Please!' I banged on the window, but she didn't even look up. Just started the ignition and put on the headlights. Then she was reversing off the forecourt and driving away and it felt as if my whole world was shattering. The past and the present were merging into one overwhelming sense of loss.

I sagged against the front door. Losing her the first time had been agonising, but it was nothing like this. I had never known anything like this pain.

★ ★ ★

At a quarter to eight, George and Mabel, the hotel's last remaining guests, came back. I knew what time it was because I was sitting in the dining room, my gaze alternating between the window and the clock. I hadn't been able to bring myself to do anything. Ever since Caroline had left, I'd sat and prayed she would come back, or at least phone me. But she hadn't done either. Now Mabel and George were cooing and waving at me through the window. For a few moments I just stared at them. Then I went to let them in, opening the door so that a gust of cold air bowled into the hall.

Mabel was wearing one of those silly hats with pull-down fluffy earmuffs and her eyes in her brown, wrinkled face were bright with excitement. Behind her, George was carrying an umbrella and several green paper shopping bags with the name of a local department store emblazoned in gold across them.

'Are you all right, dear?' Mabel hesitated in the doorway. 'Only we were waving for a long time and you didn't seem to see us.'

'That's because it's dark out there,' George said. 'We could see Joanna because she was sitting in the light, but she couldn't see us.' He peered at me and added in a stage whisper, 'Sorry, forgot our key.'

'Don't worry,' I said, fifteen years of 'be nice to guests' autopilot coming to my rescue. 'Have you had a nice day?'

Mabel nodded. 'We've had a lovely time, thanks, dear. Haven't we, George? We've just had our supper in that nice little bistro place in The Square. You know, the one with the glass lift that sells coffee in those individual pots. They're doing a special deal for Christmas shoppers and we've done all ours, haven't we, dear? Even Harold, and he's so hard to buy for.' Mabel turned back towards her husband, as I did automatically.

He coughed. 'Let's get in, shall we? It's freezing out here.' His blue eyes twinkled. Their happiness seemed so incongruous that I almost burst into tears again, but some strange numbness carried me through. Then they were in and toddling towards the stairs. George gestured for his wife to go ahead of him and they went up, still chattering. I felt excluded and lonelier than before they'd come back.

I went into the kitchen. I could phone Gail and tell her what had happened. She'd come round straight away, I knew she would, but all I really wanted was to speak to Caroline. We couldn't leave it like this. I would have phoned her except, of course, I didn't have her number. We hadn't got that far. What if she never called me back? I blinked away the thought. She'd been just as upset as I was. She wouldn't want to leave it like this. I stood by the phone, willing it to ring. Then I saw the card that Ian Sanderson from Reunited had given me, pinned to the cork noticeboard. He might not tell me where she was, but he could speak to her on my behalf. I got the card down with unsteady fingers and promptly dropped it on the tiled kitchen floor, where it slid undemeath the plate cupboard. I was just scrabbling about trying to reach it when I heard George calling from reception.

'Joanna, dear, I don't suppose we could have some more tea bags?'

Before I could stop him, he'd poked his head round the kitchen door. 'Oh dear, are you all right? Have you dropped a contact lens? Mabel's always doing that.'

'I'm fine,' I muttered, retrieving Ian's

card along with a handful of fluff and waving away George's offers of help. If he bent down any further with his dodgy hip, he'd never get up again. I fetched him his tea-bags and he thanked me profusely, then I ran back to the phone and peered at the number on the card. A mobile, so someone might even answer it. I didn't think I could face leaving a message and waiting until tomorrow.

Ian answered on the fourth ring.

'It's Joanna Cartwright here,' I said. 'You called round to see me this morning about Caroline.'

'Oh yes. How can I help?' He sounded businesslike and professional, and for a moment I didn't know what to say. I should have planned something out before I'd dialled.

'I, er . . . I need to speak to you about Caroline,' I began, and to my dismay I couldn't carry on. My voice was coming out in fits and starts.

'I'm not far from you, as it happens,' he said, not sounding at all surprised that I wanted to speak to him. 'I could

45

pop by on my way home if you like?'

I nodded, relief and tears making it impossible to reply.

'Are you still there?'

'Yes, fine,' I managed.

'See you in about ten minutes, then.'

I went and splashed cold water on my face and redid my make-up. I didn't look too bad, just a bit bright-eyed. George and Mabel hadn't noticed anything amiss. But then George was a man and Mabel was as short-sighted as me, even with her contact lenses. Besides, I only needed to see Ian Sanderson for long enough to persuade him to phone Caroline. I could hold myself together for that long.

Twenty minutes later he was sitting opposite me in the kitchen. Things weren't going to plan. Far from being calm and reasonable, all I'd managed to do so far was cry my eyes out.

I'd been fine when I'd let him in. Fine until he'd said, 'Did Caroline phone you? Is everything OK?' There had been such concern in his voice that

I'd felt myself unraveling. The next thing I knew, tears were pouring down my face.

'I'm sorry. You must think me a complete idiot,' I stammered, when I'd finally managed to stop for long enough to say something.

'It's fine. Don't worry.' He seemed unfazed by my tears and again it struck me that he must be used to this. I went and got a box of tissues from the shower room, and when I came back he said gently, 'So what went wrong?'

'Just about everything. She hates me. I don't think I'm ever going to see her again.'

'I'm sure she doesn't. It's a very emotional time, that's all.'

'No, you don't understand — she was so angry.' I told him what had happened and somehow, in the telling, calm seeped back into me and I knew I wouldn't cry again.

'I still don't think she hates you,' he repeated when I'd finished. 'She's just upset and shocked. She'll be fine when she calms down.'

'Will you phone her for me?'

'Not today. Look, you're going to have to trust me on this. Phoning her now isn't going to help.' He stood up and came round to sit beside me. 'Give her a few days. You'll need to talk to Robbie, won't you? And your husband. Then, if she hasn't phoned, I'll call her for you. How's that?'

I nodded, registering with some distant part of my mind that the front door had just slammed — Mabel and George going for a late evening stroll on the prom. I looked back at Ian Sanderson. 'Thank you.'

He touched my arm. The light, reassuring touch that one friend might give another. 'It'll be all right. Don't worry.'

I smiled at him and at that moment the door opened and Mike walked into the kitchen. He looked first at Ian Sanderson, then at me, his expression changing from surprise to wariness to incredulity.

'So Robbie wasn't messing about,' he said, his face flushing a dull red. 'I think you'd better tell me what's going on, Jo.'

3

I stared at Mike. His face was such a picture that for one crazy moment I was tempted to laugh. The next, I was spurred into anger because I could see exactly what he thought. He thought I'd been carrying on with Ian Sanderson. How he imagined I'd had either the time or inclination to start another relationship when he'd only moved out a fortnight ago was beyond me. It was ludicrous, yet I could see it in his eyes.

'So what exactly has Robbie been telling you?' I said, although I had a pretty good idea. Our well-meaning but naïve son had more or less accused me of having an affair when I'd seen him earlier.

Mike looked at Ian, who'd stood up when he'd come into the kitchen. I glanced at him too and I could see he'd read Mike's face as easily as I had. I hoped fervently that he wouldn't react to the accusation there. The last thing I wanted was to alienate the man who was the only link to my daughter.

'Well,' I said, turning back to my husband. 'Before we have any more misunderstandings, I think I should tell you that Mr Sanderson is here on behalf of our daughter. You know, Caroline — the one you'd rather forget we had.' I could hear my voice trembling with anger. 'She's been round this evening. In fact, you've only just missed her.'

Mike didn't speak, just shook his head a couple of times. He'd always avoided confrontations and now, having found himself in the middle of one, he was obviously regretting it. His face had gone a funny colour, white with two red blotches of emotion marking his cheeks. I realised with a little start of pain that the news of our daughter turning up was more of a shock to him than if I had been having an affair.

Ian handed him a business card with a slight nod.

Mike stared at it for a few seconds, before crumpling it in his hand and throwing it on to the floor.

'That isn't going to help,' I said bitterly. 'You can't carry on pretending she doesn't exist.'

Beside me, Ian gave a quiet cough and said, 'I'd better leave you to it, then.'

I glanced at him in panic. 'But you will phone Caroline for me? I mean, if . . . '

'Yes. I will. Don't worry, I'll see myself out.'

Then he was gone and it was just Mike and me. Without looking at me, Mike walked across the kitchen, slumped on to a stool at the breakfast bar and put his head in his hands.

'So are you going to say anything at all, then?' Frustration was rising in me, as it had done so many other times, because this was always Mike's answer — to switch off, withdraw into himself, like a tortoise retreating into its shell until the danger's passed.

'Does Robbie know?' he said at last. Again I felt a little stab of pain that it hadn't occurred to him to ask how I felt. All he was worried about was his son finding out he'd lied to him all these years.

'He came round when she was here. So they've met — yes. But no, he doesn't know she's his sister. We're going to have to tell him, though. We can't keep it from him now.'

He pressed his fingers to his temples. 'I've got a headache.'

'Join the club.'

'Why didn't you tell me, Jo?' He looked at me and somehow that look held the accusations of years, as if all of this was in some way my fault.

I didn't answer. I felt tired and a bit sick, the shock of the day turning into a weariness that was creeping through me like lead. All I wanted to do was to crawl into bed. Having Caroline reject me after all these years had been enough, more than enough for one day. I couldn't deal with any more.

'You should have phoned me,' Mike said.

'There wasn't time.' With the weariness had come a strange sense of calmness, but there was something I had to know. 'Do you want to meet her? Do you want to meet Caroline?'

'I don't know.' His voice was almost inaudible.

There was nothing I could have said that I wouldn't have regretted later. I went out of the kitchen, through the narrow utility room, past the freezers and washing-machines and the vacuum-cleaner and mops, past all our life together. I half expected Mike to follow me and in that moment I would have given him one last chance if he'd just tried to understand. But he didn't come.

In our bedroom I sat at the dressing-table and took the grips out of my hair. My reflection in the mirror was very pale. How had we come to this? Perhaps I should have told him what had happened when I'd seen Caroline, but I couldn't have borne to see relief on his face at something that had caused me such pain.

After a few moments I put out the light and got into bed. There were no sounds from the kitchen. For a while I lay awake in the darkness, listening to the radiators clicking. Then sleep must have come, because the next thing I knew the alarm was summonsing me to get up and prepare breakfast for my two remaining guests.

They were going home today and they were the last guests ever, I thought, with a sense of anticlimax as I made their tea and toast. Mike hadn't left a note. I was partly pleased, partly relieved. He was supposed to be meeting the developer here this morning, but I didn't have to hang around.

Once George and Mabel had left, I'd go out too. Then I wouldn't have to bump into him.

''Morning, dear,' Mabel said, when I took in their tea and asked them what they'd like for breakfast.

'Full English, please,' George said.

'We thought we'd go for a nice walk on the beach, as it's our last day. Such a beautiful one, too.'

'Good idea.' I glanced out of the window. The sky was that pale, icy blue of winter.

'We've had such a lovely time, haven't we, Mabel?'

She nodded. 'We always have a lovely time here. It's the difference, we think, between family-run hotels and big concerns. You and your husband work so hard. How's that lovely son of yours? We haven't seen him much lately.'

'Robbie's moved into a flat,' I murmured. 'You know how kids are. Can't wait to be independent.'

They exchanged glances and Mabel said, 'We weren't blessed with any children, were we, love?'

George put his hand on my arm and said, 'It's our golden wedding anniversary next year. We'd like to book up, if we may?'

Then I had to tell them there wouldn't be a next year for us. As they exclaimed their disappointment, I swallowed an ache in my throat and wondered what it must be like to be married for as long as they had and still be so obviously in love.

★   ★   ★

After breakfast I waved them off in a chorus of goodbyes and good lucks for the future. Then I phoned my best friend, Gail, and gave her a scaled-down version of the events of the previous evening. She was round within half an hour. Her familiar scent filled the kitchen as she fussed about making coffee and wiping down work surfaces.

'You look worn out,' she said, when I protested.

'I'm all right now. Or I will be when I've sorted things out with Caroline. I couldn't bear to lose her again.'

She stopped mid-wipe and frowned at me. 'But at least you can contact her — or this Ian chap can. So whatever happens you're not going to lose touch completely, are you?'

I sipped my coffee. 'I don't suppose you fancy a walk on the beach, do you, Gail?' I suggested. 'I've been cooped up in this place for weeks. I don't want to be here when Mike comes round.'

She looked ruefully at her suede shoes.

'OK, the prom, then,' I said. 'As befitting the middle-aged women that we are.'

'Speak for yourself.' She grinned. 'Yes, all right, then. I suppose we can wrap up warm.'

I fetched my coat and Gail adjusted the warm scarf at her neck, her blonde hair bouncing around her shoulders. We went out into the chill November air. Our breath puffed around us as we walked down the hill towards the pier. As we got closer to the beach, we could see that the tide was out, the sand stretching in a sweep of dull gold towards the glittering sea.

'You know, you could always come and stay with me if you like,' Gail said, as we walked past the beach huts and the brightly painted seaside café, all closed up now for the winter.

'But what if Caroline rings?'

'Well, after she's rung, then. I mean, you've only got to wait a few days, then if you haven't heard from her you can get that chap to ring up.'

'Yes.' I thought briefly of Ian Sanderson. I probably ought to phone and apologise for what had happened the previous evening. I was sure that mopping up relatives' tears and being polite to ranting husbands went far beyond the call of duty.

'So will you and Mike tell Robbie together?'

'I think Mike would rather carry on pretending this hasn't happened,' I told her.

'But he can't now, surely?' Her face was flushed pink with cold. 'Whatever happens you need to tell him soon, don't you, Jo? You can't leave it any longer.'

For a while we walked in silence. Now and then the wind swirled sand

59

along the deserted promenade. There was something very peaceful about a winter beach. I could have walked for miles, but eventually Gail said her feet were killing her and could we go back.

I smiled at her. We were so unalike, Gail and I, yet she'd always been there for me, despite the fact she'd never had any children of her own. I suddenly felt immensely touched.

'Once we've sold the hotel I'm going to have a break,' I told her. 'Maybe go and do something exotic, like climb up Mount Kilimanjaro in Africa. Fancy coming?'

She laughed and shook her head. 'You'll be much too busy being a grandma.'

I reached for her hand. 'Do you really think that will happen?'

'I don't see why not.'

Back in the warmth of the hotel kitchen, I found a note from Mike saying the property developer had made an offer and he'd talk to me later.

'Nothing about Robbie. I'm going to

have to phone him, aren't I?'

'Ring me later and tell me how it goes. And don't forget what I said about coming to stay.' We hugged.

When she'd gone, I called Robbie and asked him to come round later that day.

'I'm a bit busy, Mum,' he said. 'Can it wait until later in the week?'

'No, it can't, love. It's important.'

'Is it to do with you and Dad? Can't you tell me now?'

'Yes it is and no, I don't want to discuss it on the phone. Please, Robbie. I'll make you some tea.'

'Sunday roast?'

'Well, yes, I suppose so.'

'Oh, don't bother if it's too much trouble,' he sighed. 'I'll pop by about six, then.'

I put down the phone and set about peeling potatoes, thinking ruefully that Robbie probably wouldn't be speaking to me by the end of the evening, so it might be the last chance I'd get for a while.

He turned up at ten past six. 'Something smells good,' he murmured. 'So what's so important that you can't tell me about it on the phone?'

'I thought we could eat in the dining room,' I said quickly, sidestepping the question.

'Just the two of us? Or are you expecting someone else?'

'No, Robbie, I'm not.' I looked at him in exasperation. 'What did you tell your father yesterday? He came round last night.'

'Just that you were acting strangely. Well, you were.' He had the grace to blush as he bent and kissed me. 'I'm sorry, Mum. I didn't mean to wind Dad up. What did he say?'

His blue eyes were troubled and I felt myself softening. 'Nothing much. Your father never says much, does he? Fancy a glass of wine with dinner?'

'Yeah, just the one, then.' He grinned. 'I'll lay up, shall I?'

'Thanks,' When I carried in our plates, I saw that Robbie had lit a candle and put it in the centre of one of the tables. My stomach crunched with nerves. I'd been thinking about it all afternoon, but I still hadn't worked out how to make my news less of a shock.

'So what are we celebrating?' Robbie said, tucking into his beef, while I picked at mine. 'Have you sold this place?'

'It's looking good. A developer has made an offer.'

'You won't know what to do with yourself, will you?' His eyes were bright and I thought of grandchildren and felt a little rush of guilt.

'I'll find something, I expect.' He'd almost finished his dinner now. I couldn't put off the moment forever. 'Your dad and I . . . ' I began, but before I could continue, Robbie said, 'It's all right, Mum. I know I haven't been very fair. Dad phoned me this afternoon. He told me it was a mutual decision, you splitting up. That I couldn't blame it all on you.'

'He did?' I looked at Robbie in

astonishment. 'Did he say anything else to you?'

'No, but it's funny — I had the feeling he wanted to,' Robbie answered. 'You know how Dad is.'

I nodded, amazed that Mike had said anything at all. Up until now it seemed that he'd been quite happy to let Robbie think he was the injured party. It must have cost him dear, admitting he was partly to blame.

Robbie wiped his mouth with a paper serviette. 'So I'm sorry, Mum. If you and Dad are really sure, then I guess I'll have to accept it too. It's not like there's anyone else involved, is there? We can still all be friends, can't we?'

'Of course we can.' My voice had gone a bit husky. I'd always known the moment would come when I realised my son was becoming an adult. But why did it have to be now? Just when I was about to give him the greatest shock of his life.

'So what did you want to tell me?' Robbie finished his wine. 'Was it the same thing Dad was going to say?'

'Very possibly,' I said, thinking that I might even be right. Maybe Mike had meant to mention Caroline but hadn't found the courage. I couldn't blame him. I was finding it hard enough.

'There's no easy way to tell you, love, so I'm just going to come straight out with it,' I began.

Robbie looked at me, his eyes expectant. 'Well, come on then, it can't be that bad.'

'I hope you won't think it's bad at all. The fact is, you've got a sister. An older sister we've never told you about. We had her adopted three years before you were born.'

For a few seconds Robbie didn't say anything. He just looked at me, his blue eyes almost blank, a tiny frown creasing his forehead. Then he put down his empty wine glass and said, 'Can you just run that by me again, Mum? I don't think I'm quite with you.'

'You've got a sister,' I said, feeling the words catch in my throat. 'I'm so sorry

we haven't told you before. I . . . we
. . . well, we wanted to, but there just
never seemed to be a right time.'

He'd gone very still. He stared at his
plate and I wished Mike were here.
Wished I wasn't doing this on my own.

'Are you saying you had a baby
before you met Dad? I mean, when you
were too young to keep it — her?' Then
he did look at me again, his face a
strange mixture of shock and pain.
'Does Dad know? I mean, is this why
you've split up?'

'No. No, love. Look, I'm not
explaining it properly. Just after I met
your dad, I fell pregnant, but we weren't
married. I was barely eighteen. We thought
adoption was the best thing to do for
the baby, for Caroline.'

'Caroline?' Shock filled his voice
and, too late, I realised my mistake.
'You mean Caroline, that girl who was
here yesterday?'

I nodded silently. Every muscle in my
body felt tense. I couldn't imagine how
he must be feeling.

'Robbie, love, I know this must be a huge shock.' I reached for his hand, but he snatched it away.

'Damn right it's a shock.' As he stood up, he knocked the table, clattering the cutlery on our plates and causing the candle to flicker wildly. He walked across to the dining room window and stood looking out into the cold winter darkness. I could see his face, dark and angry, reflected in one of the big mirrors by the window.

I wanted to go to him, to hug him and tell him everything was going to be all right, like I had when he was a little boy, but I knew there was nothing I could say that wouldn't just twist the knife in the wound. Resentment towards Mike welled up inside me again. He should have been here helping me to deal with this. But then, if he'd ever helped me deal with it we wouldn't have split up, I realised with sudden, bitter insight. Our entire marriage had been blighted by this secret, by him refusing to acknowledge Caroline, refusing to discuss her with me or with Robbie. Now our son was bearing the brunt of the pain and in that moment I hated Mike for putting us in this situation.

I got up and went across to where Robbie stood. He didn't look at me, but his face was bleak.

'I'd never met Caroline before yesterday. I'd always hoped she'd get in touch, but . . . '

'Why didn't you tell me yesterday? God, I can't believe you didn't tell me then. You just let me blunder in, didn't you?' His voice was savage with pain. 'But she knew who I was, didn't she? What were you doing? Laughing at me because I didn't know?'

'No, of course not. Love, I'm so sorry. The last thing I wanted was for you to find out like this.'

'So how did you want me to find out? And more to the point, when?' He stepped away from me as if he couldn't bear to be near me. 'Or perhaps you were never going to mention it. It was just to be your little secret. Yours and Dad's.'

'No, Robbie. Of course we would have told you.'

'Do you know what hurts the most?' he continued, as if I hadn't spoken. 'I've always pitied my mates who haven't got fathers. I thought it must be terrible never knowing your dad. I always thought that Dad and me were close, but we're not, are we? I don't know him at all.' His voice broke and I shook my head helplessly.

'Of course you do. You are close.'

'Yeah, right.' He folded his arms. 'Is there anything else you'd like to mention? Any other little secrets you want to confess?'

'No, of course not.'

He went and picked up his jacket from the back of his chair.

'Where are you going?'

'Does it matter?' He shrugged it on and headed for the door.

'Robbie!'

He hesitated. 'I'm going to see Dad. I'm going to see what he's got to say about all this.'

'Then let me come with you.'

'I don't think so.'

I followed him out into the hallway. 'Please drive carefully, Robbie.'

He didn't answer, just went out into the darkness, slamming the front door, and I knew with an aching sense of loss that it would be stupid to try and follow him. I had to let him go, to sort everything out in his mind. At least he wasn't on his motor bike. When he'd moved out, Mike and I had bought him a car and paid for the tax and insurance so we wouldn't have to worry about him riding around on a bike. I'd never been more glad of it than I was now.

I went back into the dining room. The candle Robbie had lit earlier glowed above our dirty plates. I blew it out and watched the haze of smoke dissipate. I couldn't cry. I was all cried out Robbie's reaction hadn't been a surprise. I was more surprised that I felt quite calm. There was a stillness inside me that took a while to place, and then I realised it was relief. The secret I'd kept for so long was well and truly out in the open. Whatever happened now, there was no going back. We all had to move on, adjust to this new future — whatever it might bring.

4

Three days later, my best friend Gail and I were sitting in the hotel kitchen drinking tea, while I gave her an update on everything that had happened since the weekend. I still hadn't heard any more from Caroline, but Mike and Robbie had both been round to visit the previous day, although not together.

'Robbie's still furious with his father,' I told Gail, 'and Mike's really upset. He's never had to cope with anything like this before.'

'How about you?' she asked gently. 'How are you coping with it all? Are you still angry with Mike, too?'

I shook my head. 'No, it's odd, isn't it? I never thought I'd say it, but I almost feel sorry for him. I can't be cross with him any more.'

'Not sorry enough to have him back?' she asked, stirring her tea and pushing the plate of biscuits I'd put beside her to the other end of the table.

'Feeling sorry for someone isn't much basis for staying married to them, is it?'

'No, I guess not. Still it's early days. With Robbie, I mean,' she said, catching my look. 'It's been a huge shock for him.'

'Yes,' I said, thinking about Robbie. I guess I shouldn't have been surprised that he was acting as he was towards Mike. He'd always idolised his father, put him on a pedestal. Mike had had a lot further to fall than me. I'd always had a much more down-to-earth relationship with our son.

'So are you going to phone that chap from the agency?' Gail asked, studying me. 'He said he'd phone Caroline for you, didn't he, if you hadn't heard from her?'

'Yes, I will.' I thought guiltily of Ian Sanderson from Reunited. I'd meant to phone him before and apologise for Mike's behaviour. If I was honest, one

73

of the reasons I hadn't was because I'd been too embarrassed. Not because of Mike's insinuation that we were having some sort of affair, but because I'd gone to pieces in front of him. Cried my heart out because the daughter I'd dreamed of meeting for so long had rejected me so thoroughly. I rarely cried in front of close friends and family, let alone a complete stranger. The other reason I hadn't phoned him was Caroline. If she told Ian she didn't want to see me again, then I'd have nothing left. This way I still had hope.

'Anyway, enough about me,' I said to Gail. 'Tell me all your news. You haven't told me what's going on in your life for ages.'

'That's because nothing is,' she said, sipping her tea and raising her eyebrows. 'Unless you want to know about my dishwasher breaking down, or the man who's moved in next door now that Judy and Bill have emigrated to France.'

'Well, the man next door sounds

promising. Anyone interesting?' I gave her a meaningful glance and she smiled.

'Not in the way you mean. His name's Eric and he's at least eighty.'

'And there was I thinking you were going to brighten up my day with some gossip about a new man in your life!'

'Afraid not.' She sighed then and dragged the biscuit plate back again. 'You should put these away before I eat them all.'

'Feel free.'

'I can't eat as much as I like and stay slim like you can.' She sighed again broke the corner off a digestive and popped it in her mouth. 'I wouldn't mind a bit of romance actually, Jo, but there aren't many nice men around when you get to our age. All the ones I meet are either confirmed bachelors or they're married and just want a quick fling behind their wives' backs. Not that I want a major commitment again,' she added hastily. 'I'd just like a nice, intelligent, sensitive man. Preferably one who wants me for my body and not my money.'

I smiled. 'It can't be that difficult. Tell you what. Once this place is sold, you and I can go out and paint the town red.'

'You mean go clubbing? I think not! Since when do you meet any intelligent, sensitive men out clubbing?'

'OK then, what about a dating agency? Or we could put an ad in the newspaper. You could, anyway. I've got to get divorced first. I could help you sift through the replies. It'd keep us entertained for an evening.'

She grimaced. 'Yes, I can see it now. Blonde forty-something divorcee seeks caring man for fun times.'

'You'd be inundated, Gail.'

'Yes, but with what? I can't even rely on you any more to phone me up when you've got any promising guests in. How's the sale going anyway?'

'Stop changing the subject.'

'I'm not.' She picked up the rest of the biscuit and dunked it in what was left of her tea. 'I'm interested.'

'Well, we've accepted the developer's

offer. He wants a completion date for early December and Mike's already fixed up, so the only thing that's likely to hold us up is me finding somewhere.'

'Don't forget what I said about staying with me. You know I'd love to have you.'

'Thanks. I know. I might take you up on that. But I've really got to sort out something permanent. I've been so up in the air these last few days, I've hardly given it a thought.' I stood up. 'Want some more tea?'

'No, I'd better get going. I've got the dishwasher repair man coming round.' She was just reaching for her coat and scarf when the doorbell rang. 'Are you expecting anyone?'

I frowned. 'No. Could be Robbie again, or Mike. He's always finding some excuse to pop round.'

Gail walked ahead of me along the hallway. 'Talking of interesting men,' she called over her shoulder, 'the one on your doorstep doesn't look bad. Pity you're closed. I could have stayed a bit longer and checked him out.'

'That's Ian Sanderson,' I said, as we got closer to the glass front door. Hope was fizzing inside me. He could only be here for one reason: news from Caroline.

'Well, you never told me he looked like that.' Gail squeezed my hand. 'Hope it's good news, love. I'll ring you later.'

Then I was opening the door and Ian stood back a little to let Gail by. She fluttered her eyelashes at him and he smiled. Then he turned to me. 'Say if I've called at a bad time.'

'No, not at all.' I waved at Gail over his shoulder. 'Come in. I've been meaning to phone you.'

He followed me into the kitchen.

'Would you like a coffee? The kettle's just boiled.'

'No, I won't hold you up.'

The last time he'd had coffee with me, Mike had barged in and jumped to the wrong conclusion. No wonder he wasn't keen, I thought wryly. 'Look, I'm really sorry about the other night,' I said. 'That's why I was going to phone you — to apologise. It's just that emotions are running a bit high at the moment. Mike didn't really think . . . '

'It's all right. I've been accused of all sorts of things in my time.' His voice was warm, but he still didn't sit down.

'Really?'

'You'd be amazed,' he answered. 'Anyway, I came round to tell you that Caroline phoned me this morning. It's good news. She's had a think and she doesn't want to leave things as they are. She wants to see you again.'

'Brilliant! Brilliant,' I said, relief flooding me through me like a tidal wave. 'Oh, thank you so much for coming round. I'm so pleased.'

'Me too.' He looked it. 'How are you?'

'I'm fine.' I hesitated. 'I've told Robbie about Caroline. Are you sure you won't have coffee?'

'Oh, go on then.' He sat on the stool at the breakfast bar. 'How did it go?'

His voice was gentle and I bit my lip. Funny how kindness can tip you into tears when you're feeling emotional, but the last thing I wanted to do was break down in front of this man again.

'He was angry, furious that we hadn't told him.'

'That'll pass.'

'Will it? I don't blame him for being angry. All his life we've brought him up believing he's an only child and now we've sprung this on him. I wouldn't blame him if he never trusted us again.' I broke off. What was it about Ian that made it so easy to tell him things? 'I'm sorry,' I said. 'I'm going on at you again, aren't I?'

'No, you're not Look, I do understand how you feel.'

'No you don't. You can't.' I looked into his strong, kind face and thought Gail was right, he was attractive; but it was more to do with his air of calmness than anything physical. And that was just professionalism, I thought. 'Look, what I mean is I know you see this all the time — it's your job, isn't it? — but you can't know how I feel. How Robbie feels.'

'Yes I can,' he said quietly. 'I'm adopted myself. My parents didn't tell me until I was thirty-four, and then they didn't mean to. It came out in a family argument.' His voice was still calm, but his eyes were darker. 'I was angry, furious with them. I felt betrayed. It's not easy finding out all your past history is a lie.'

I blinked a couple of times. It was all starting to make sense. His kindness, his empathy. 'Is that why you started doing this?' I asked. 'Putting families in touch with each other?'

'Yes. I tried everything to trace my birth mother. The Salvation Army, even a private investigator. By the time I tracked her down it was too late. She'd died three months earlier.' He paused. 'It's easier now. There's the Internet. The world's a lot smaller, but at the time I thought that maybe if there was a proper agency, somewhere that really cared, then people — families — might have more chance. This is more than a job to me. It's my passion.'

I could see that he meant it. 'What about your father?' I said softly. 'Did you find him?'

'I did.' He paused and went on without bitterness, 'He didn't want to know. Had a new family. A new life. Didn't want a past mistake fouling things up for him.'

I closed my eyes.

Ian cleared his throat and said, 'It's OK. It was a long time ago. But you see, I do understand a little of how Robbie feels, and Caroline. And I can see how you feel. You love them both very much. That's a good start. I think it's going to be all right, Mrs Cartwright. I really do.'

'It's Jo,' I said.

He smiled. 'I'm sure Caroline will call you soon. Robbie will calm down. He's very young. You just need to give them time. That's the best advice I can give you. If you want to talk, you know where I am.'

Impulsively, I reached for his hand and squeezed it. 'Thank you.' There was a lot I wanted to talk to him about, but I didn't know where to start. He made me feel strangely vulnerable, this man. Then I realised, with a flash of insight, that it wasn't him. I felt vulnerable now simply because I could be. For years I'd had to be the strong one, the one who'd put on the brave face. Keeping my pain about Caroline hidden from both Mike and Robbie. But there was no need for pretence any more. I could show my emotions, take them out and air them in the light of day, just as I'd taken out Caroline's clothes from the dusty suitcase in the box room upstairs. It was a new sensation.

'Anyway,' Ian said, 'I've got an appointment, so I'd better be off.'

'Thank you,' I said again, getting up to see him out.

'My pleasure. And good luck,' he said, as we stood at the front door once more.

That afternoon, Caroline telephoned. I recognised her voice as soon as I picked up the phone.

'I'm so sorry about the other night,' I said. 'I truly didn't mean for Robbie to turn up. For things to turn out like they did.'

'No, it's me who should be apologising.'

She sounded breathless, shy, and my heart turned over at the sound of her voice. Since that first meeting had gone so wrong, I'd tried not to think about her. It was the only way I could cope. But now it was flooding back again, that tumult of fear and hope.

'I'd no right to judge you like that,' she went on softly. 'I don't suppose . . . well, I don't suppose we could start again, could we?'

'There's nothing I'd like more.'

'I thought maybe if we met on neutral territory this time? There's a pub by the pier where we could eat — The Seahorse, I think it's called. I could meet you there, if you like.'

'You mean after work?'

She laughed. 'I'm on maternity leave, so any time you like.'

'Of course.' I realised with a jolt that I didn't even know when her baby was due. There was so much I didn't know about her, so many aching gaps to fill.

'I thought about four?' Caroline said. 'Does that give you enough time, or do you have to cook dinner for guests and things?'

'No, we're closed.' I reflected that there was so much Caroline didn't know about me too. Impossible to fit a lifetime into an hour or two at The Seahorse, but it was a start. A beginning.

'Four o'clock will be perfect,' I said.

I had been given a second chance, I thought, as I put the phone down. Or a third one, depending on how you looked at it. This time it would be perfect. This time nothing would go wrong.

I had two hours to kill before our meeting. For some reason I found myself upstairs on the top landing, looking at the outfits I'd bought in secret for Caroline, one for every year of her life. They were still hung round the banisters where I'd left them after I'd shown Gail. I hadn't been able to bring myself to look at them again, let alone put them away. Besides, it hardly mattered now. There was no one in the hotel to see them. Robbie hadn't mentioned them again. Neither had Mike, I realised, although he must have noticed them when he'd shown the property developer around.

I picked up the one that was closest to Caroline's age now. An ivory silk suit that a twenty-one-year-old might wear on a posh night out. I held the soft material up against my face, breathing in its newness. It was a size ten. I hadn't been far off the mark there, although of course it wouldn't have fitted her at the moment.

Then, on impulse, I picked up the first outfit I'd ever bought for her. The pink romper-suit, age up to six months. Did romper-suits go out of date? Anyway, she might have a boy, and she might think it presumptuous if I turned up with this for her baby. Unable to decide, I held it against my body. A roller-coaster of emotions was tumbling through me, but the main one, the overriding one, was joy. I was so lucky, so very, very lucky to be given another chance.

* * *

By half-past three I'd changed my mind about what to wear a dozen times. I knew it was ridiculous. Caroline knew what I looked like, but I so wanted it to be right this time. In the end, I decided on my smart white jeans and a fleece. The little pink romper-suit was in a carrier bag in the hallway. Should I take it or not? At the last minute I decided not to and left it where it was by the door. I'd buy a brand-new romper-suit and a teddy bear and everything in the world if I were allowed to be part of my new grandchild's life.

I checked my reflection for the last

time and went out into the November evening. As I shut the front door, a car pulled up on to the forecourt. Mike's car. I hesitated as he got out of it.

'Hi, Jo.'

He looked at me quizzically and I felt bound to say something. 'I'm just popping out.'

'Can I give you a lift?' He locked the car door and came round towards me. 'Going anywhere nice?'

For a moment I was tempted to lie to him, but then I thought, no, there'd been enough secrets and anyway, there was no reason not to tell him where I was going.

'I'm going to see Caroline at The Seahorse,' I said, meeting his eyes steadily. 'She phoned me this afternoon.'

'I see.' His blue eyes were troubled and I waited for him to shrug and say, 'Good luck,' or some other platitude, but he didn't, just jangled the keys in his hand. 'I . . . well, I don't suppose I could come with you, could I?'

'Come with me?'

Shock must have reached my voice because he said, 'Well, I am her dad — or is it too soon? I mean, maybe she wouldn't want to see me. Look, why don't I give you a lift down there and we can talk about it on the way?'

'But it's only down the road.'

'Please, Jo.' Something in his voice stopped me in my tracks. It was the first time he'd ever acknowledged we had a daughter, let alone any desire to meet her. He was right, he was her dad. Who was I to say he couldn't come? A few seconds later we were driving down the hill towards the beach.

'I don't mind waiting in the car,' he murmured, as he parked in the car park overlooking the sea, the lights of The Seahorse behind us. He sounded unsure of himself, almost vulnerable.

I glanced at him. 'I think it might be best, Mike, if you don't mind. She's only expecting me and I don't want anything to go wrong.'

I'd given Mike the sketchiest of

details about what had happened the first time I'd met Caroline. He hadn't said much and it had been impossible to work out what he'd been thinking. It was just as impossible now. He rested his elbows on the steering wheel, his face in shadow.

'I'll tell her you're out here,' I went on gently. 'So she can decide.'

'OK.'

As I got out, he added, 'Hope it goes well, Jo.'

I shut the car door and looked at the sea. The sun was just sinking below the horizon, turning the sky pink and casting a glittering path across the waves. It looked beautiful, a good omen, and I realised it was the first time in ages I'd felt positive about the future. Felt that somehow, out of all this mess, things were going to come right.

As I walked towards the welcoming lights of the pub, I wondered if Caroline was already waiting for me inside. I opened the door on to warmth and brightness. It was the sort of place that serves food all day, mainly to tourists. A big, impersonal pub and no one's local. Fishnets were strung from the ceilings, filled with pink plastic lobsters and crabs. Along one wall, windows overlooked the sea. On another, a giant mural of a seahorse was painted. There weren't many people about, which I supposed wasn't surprising at only just gone four.

I walked round all the nooks and crannies, but there was no sign of Caroline, so I bought myself an orange juice, found a table by the window in sight of the door and sat down. As I waited, I wondered what had brought about Mike's change of heart — or had it just been a spur of the moment decision? Maybe even now he was sitting out there regretting it. I thought about what Gail had said about me having him back, but that wasn't a train of thought I wanted to pursue.

At twenty past four, I began to wonder if Caroline had definitely said The Seahorse. I was sure she had, but in my excitement my relief, could I possibly have got it wrong? At her request, I'd given her my mobile number in case she was held up. I checked it was switched on.

The hands of my watch crept slowly round to five and the sea outside the windows darkened to steely grey, then black. One by one, the lights on the prom came on and I realised that Caroline wasn't coming.

This was beginning to feel like some sort of awful nightmare At ten past five, I got up and walked round the pub in case I'd somehow missed her coming in. She wasn't here. By five-fifteen I had a horrible, sick feeling of despair. I had to face it. Caroline had obviously changed her mind and decided that she didn't want to see me again after all.

5

I felt shattered, despairing, as I walked around the gaudy seaside pub one last time. It was now an hour and twenty minutes after the time I'd arranged to meet Caroline and darkness was pressing against the windows. She wasn't coming. I had to accept it, but it wasn't until I was walking in slow motion towards the exit door that I wondered if she'd ever intended to come. Perhaps she just wanted me to know what it felt like to be rejected.

I shrugged away the thought as paranoia. A part of me was still hoping she'd come dashing in before I reached the door, apologetic in a flurry of fresh air and breathlessness, explaining that someone had called round, or her car had broken down. Anything other than the fact that she just didn't want to see me.

But no one came in and I went outside into the gusty dark of the car park. Mike was still sitting in his car. I'd half-expected him to be gone. I wouldn't have blamed him. I'd promised I'd tell Caroline he was out here waiting. He must have thought she hadn't wanted to see him. He must be feeling as bad as I was. As I approached the car, he got out and came to meet me. He rubbed his hands togeher. He looked cold.

'Everything OK? How was she?'

I shook my head and swallowed a couple of times, glad of the darkness, but Mike wasn't fooled. 'You've been waiting all this time and she didn't come?'

I didn't answer and he said, in a voice that dared me to argue, 'I'll drive you back and you can tell me about it.'

We drove the short distance in silence and I wondered what I was going to say to him. And what he was going to say to me? Mike had never wanted to discuss Caroline. For the whole of our marriage he'd wanted to forget we'd ever had a daughter. Said it was for the best. Now it seemed she didn't want anything to do with us, would he say that was for the best too? I didn't think I could bear it if he did. He parked on the hotel forecourt and I got out of the car. As he came round to the front door, I said quietly, 'Maybe it's better if you don't come in, Mike.'

'I won't stop long.'

I shrugged. I was having trouble getting the front-door key in. My fingers wouldn't function properly. After a few moments of fumbling, Mike took the key from me and opened the door. As we went into the hallway, he bent to pick up the white, plastic carrier bag I'd left by the front door. Before I could stop him, he glanced inside and I knew he must have seen the pink romper suit I'd bought Caroline all those years ago. He didn't say anything, just handed the bag to me. I took it without looking at him. Tears blurred my eyes as I clutched it to my chest. If only we hadn't given her up. If only she'd had a chance to wear this, how different things might have been.

'Jo?' I felt Mike's hand on my arm.

'What?'

'You look as though you could do with a stiff drink, and I know I could.' He left me standing in the hall and went through reception. When I followed him into the kitchen he was getting the bottle of Glenfiddich out of the cupboard. He often had an after-dinner scotch in his coffee when we were really busy in the hotel, but he didn't bother with coffee now, just splashed the amber liquid into glasses. He looked tired, I thought. His face was more lined than usual, more shadowed. All this upset with Robbie had really got to him.

We took our glasses into the dining room. 'Now sit down,' he said, an unaccustomed firmness in his voice, 'and tell me what happened.'

I sipped my drink, feeling its fiery warmth in my throat. 'There's not much to say, Mike. She obviously thought better of coming. I can't blame her.'

He frowned, but he looked as though he was listening, as if he actually cared what I said, and maybe it was alcohol on an empty stomach, or maybe it was because I'd never had the opportunity to talk to him before, but the words came tumbling out. I told him everything. How much I'd missed Caroline over the years, how excited I'd been when Ian Sanderson of Reunited had told me she wanted to meet me, and then how devastated I'd felt when it had all gone wrong. 'This was another chance,' I said. 'But I've blown it, haven't I? I guess you were right all along. I should have done what you did and cut off from her years ago.' I knew I sounded bitter, but I had to say it before Mike did.

'I've missed her too,' he said, when I'd finally ground to a halt.

For a moment, I didn't think I'd heard him right. I looked into the steady blue of his eyes and he met my gaze. 'But, if that's true, Mike, why didn't you ever say anything? Why did you always clam up when I mentioned her name?'

He poured more Glenfiddich into his glass. 'I didn't think there was much point in talking about her because I didn't think we'd ever see her again. I thought it would just upset you.'

I could see the truth of what he was saying in his face, but before I could respond, he went on, 'Anyway, Jo, be honest. You were more interested in telling Robbie about Caroline than discussing her with me.'

He was right, I realised, with a little jolt of awareness. When Caroline had first been adopted, I'd just wanted to forget what we'd done. I'd never told Mike about the nightmares I'd had. Particularly those early bizarre nightmares about a baby locked in a cupboard. It had been too painful to share, even with him. Then, when we'd had Robbie, I'd wanted to tell him about his sister. Maybe I'd been unfair to Mike, expecting him to read my mind. To know the difference between that early raw hurt and the later panicky realisation that we must never forget our daughter. 'I didn't think you wanted to know,' I murmured. 'I thought you'd rather pretend she didn't exist.'

'I suppose in a way I did,' he said heavily. 'But only because I couldn't deal with it. You did the opposite, didn't you, Jo?'

'What do you mean?'

He drained his glass and looked at me. 'All those clothes upstairs. You bought them for her, didn't you?'

* * *

By ten o'clock we were both a little drunk and we'd talked more about our feelings than I could remember us ever doing before.

'You'll have to stay here. You can't drive back to the flat,' I told Mike.

'Now there's an offer I can't refuse.'

I bit my lip and he smiled ruefully. 'Don't worry, Jo. I'll sleep on the couch.'

I could hear him pottering around in the tiny lounge adjacent to our bedroom, as I got ready for bed. My head was spinning, partly from drinking too much and partly at the revelations of the evening. 'At least you've seen her once,' Mike had said. 'At least you know what she looks like, you know she's OK. That's surely got to be better than nothing, hasn't it?'

My last conscious thought before sleep came was that he was right. There would be no more dreams of babies in the cupboard. Caroline was all grown up and even if we never saw her again, at least I could take comfort in the knowledge that she was OK, that very soon she would have a family of her own to worry about.

In the morning, with no alarm to wake me, I overslept. Ten past nine. I hadn't woken so late for months. I grabbed my dressing-gown, wishing, when my head pounded, that I hadn't stood up so quickly. There were no sounds from next door and when I went in I found the duvet neatly folded on the settee and Mike gone. I swallowed a little ache of disappointment. After all, we were still selling the hotel, still getting divorced. One night of talking didn't change any of that.

In the kitchen I found a note. *Didn't want to wake you. Thanks for the use of the couch. Will phone later re developer. Mike.*

I'd just finished reading it when the telephone rang. When I picked it up, a crisply efficient voice said, 'Could I speak to Joanna Cartwright, please?'

'Speaking.'

'Hello, Mrs Cartwright. I'm calling from St Frances Maternity Hospital on behalf of Caroline Lacey. She wanted me to let you know she had an eight pound baby girl at six-thirty this morning.'

I held the phone, speechless. Mike

and I had discussed lots of things, but neither of us had considered the possibility that Caroline might have wanted to come last night but hadn't been able to.

'Are you still there, Mrs Cartwright?'

'Yes, sorry. Is she . . . are they all right?'

'They're both absolutely fine.'

I could hear the smile in the woman's voice. She reeled off the visiting hours and I wrote them down, my brain on autopilot. I still had a daughter — and I had a grandchild, too. It was only when something dropped on to the pad of paper I was writing on that I realised tears were pouring down my face.

I phoned Mike at the flat, but there was no answer. I had to tell someone, so I phoned my friend Gail at work.

'Wonderful news!' she said, when she'd finally made sense of my gabbling. 'When are you going to see them?'

'As soon as I've bought the biggest teddy I can find.'

'Brilliant.' Gail hesitated, then went on slowly, 'This does put a different

102

light on things, of course.'

'How do you mean?'

'Well, I don't see how I can embark on my hunt for the perfect man with some old granny in tow.'

'Hey, less of the old,' I said and she giggled.

'Actually, Jo, while we're on the subject of men, I wanted to ask you a favour.'

'Fire away.'

'I don't suppose I could have Ian Sanderson's number, could I? I'm going to ask him if he fancies a drink.'

'A drink?' I said.

'He can take me for a meal as well, if he likes, but I thought we'd start off with a drink.'

'You shameless hussy.'

'Why, he's not married, is he?'

'Not as far as I know.' I read the number out to her. 'Good luck.'

'You too. Give that baby a kiss for me.'

I put the phone down and took two headache tablets with a mug of tea. Then I went to the toyshop on the precinct and bought a giant teddy with a pink bow around his neck. When I explained what I wanted him for, the shopkeeper tried to sell me a bear with a card that said, *For my first grandchild*. As I looked into her smiling face, I felt the first cold rush of trepidation. Technically, Caroline's baby might be my grandchild, but if I went racing up to maternity now I might find myself face to face with another proud grandmother who had far more right to be there than I had.

As I drove back home again, with ted on the passenger seat beside me, it struck me I probably shouldn't even go to maternity today. I should leave it till tomorrow or even the day after. Until the hospital had referred to her as Caroline Lacey, I hadn't even known her surname and I knew nothing of her life now. Nothing of the people who'd brought her up. This was their celebration, their moment. The last person they'd want to bump into over Caroline's hospital bed was me.

I finally got hold of Mike about four. When he'd got over the shock of finding out he was a grandad, he said, 'Why don't you phone the hospital? I'm sure Caroline wouldn't have got them to call you if she didn't want you to visit.'

He sounded distant, as if he didn't want to be discussing Caroline, and I wondered with a pang whether last night had been a one-off. Whether he would have preferred it if Caroline had just changed her mind about meeting me.

'Are you all right, Mike?'

'I'm fine. Look, do you think I could call you back? I'm a bit tied up at the moment.'

'Yes, of course.'

I hung up and dialled the number of the maternity unit with trembling fingers.

Yes, I could speak to her, the nurse said. She'd get her to phone me back on the trolley phone in a few minutes.

I found out more about my daughter

in that five-minute conversation than I'd known for the past twenty-one years.

I found out she had a boyfriend, Nick, who worked as a motorcycle courier and had been about to set off on a trip to London when his controller had radioed him and told him to get home pronto.

'The baby was two weeks early,' Caroline explained, her voice fuzzy with tiredness and happiness. 'That's why I thought it would be OK to see you yesterday. I'm sorry about that, by the way. Did you wait very long?'

'Not too long,' I said, resolving never to tell her what I'd thought.

I found out that her adoptive parents had split up several years previously and that her mother, who she'd been closest to, had died the previous year.

'That's why I decided to contact you,' she said. 'I couldn't have done it when Mum was still alive. It would have broken her heart.'

'I can understand that,' I said, feeling

half-sad, half-relieved that I'd never meet the woman who'd brought up my little girl.

'Dad's coming in later,' Caroline went on. 'With Maureen, his new partner, but they won't stay long. Between you and me, Maureen disapproves of the fact that Nick and I aren't planning to get married.' Her voice was indignant as she went on, 'The way we see it, getting married doesn't guarantee a stable home for a child anyway. Nick's parents split up when he was ten.'

How ironic, I thought, that we'd given Caroline up because I'd thought we couldn't give her a stable background, yet Mike and I were still together. Then I remembered with a jolt that we weren't.

'You could come in the morning,' Caroline said. 'If you wanted to, I mean.'

'I'd love to,' I said.

I couldn't bear to stay in for the rest of the day, so I went round to see Gail.

She'd just come in from work when I got there. She met me at the front door, with her coat on.

'Hi, Granny,' she said, grinning. 'On your way to the hospital?'

'Tomorrow.'

We hugged and she added, 'I'm so pleased for you, love. Fancy meeting your daughter and your grandchild for the first time all in the space of a week! I wish my life was half as exciting.'

'So get the kettle on and tell me what Ian Sanderson said,' I urged her.

'What makes you think I've phoned him?' She raised her eyebrows, kicked her shoes off in the hallway, hung her coat on the coat-stand and went into her immaculate oak kitchen.

I followed breathlessly and watched her fill the kettle. 'You never hang around once you've made up your mind to do something.' I rummaged in the biscuit cupboard. 'So where are you hiding the chocolate digestives these days?'

'I'm on a diet. I've got to lose three

pounds by Saturday, so I can fit into this little black number I bought from Dorinda's at lunch-time.'

I stopped rummaging and turned round. 'Dorinda's? My goodness, where's he taking you?'

She thrust an expensive-looking carrier bag under my nose. 'What do you think?'

I unwrapped the tissue paper and drew out the dress. 'It's beautiful, Gail. So come on then, I want to know exactly what he said.'

She giggled. 'I haven't asked a man out in ages. Well, years, actually. Do you know I was shaking when I phoned him? Can you believe that?'

'Only too well,' I said, with feeling.

'He was really nice. Said he'd be delighted, as long as it was understood that he was paying. We're going to that new Thai place up the road.' She closed her eyes and smiled. I hadn't seen her looking so happy for weeks.

'That's brilliant,' I said.

'You don't think this dress is too

revealing?' She held it against her.

'No, I don't. He's a nice guy.'

'You don't mind that I'm not going to do all that man-searching stuff with you?' She made our tea and put two cups on the kitchen table. 'Anyway, you never know, we might not get on.'

'No, I don't mind. I've got loads of stuff to sort out before I get that far.' I decided now wasn't the time to tell Gail about the conversation I'd had with Mike last night, then remembered suddenly that he'd said he'd phone me back. 'I don't suppose I could use your phone, could I?'

'Feel free. You know where it is. I'll just get changed out of my work stuff. If you really want a chocolate biscuit, there's an emergency supply in the bread bin.'

While she was changing, I phoned Mike.

'I'm sorry about earlier,' he said. 'Robbie was here. We had a bit of a heart to heart.'

'How did it go?'

'Fine. Robbie gave me a load of ear-ache about not communicating, but I think we've finally sorted things out. But, Jo, I'm afraid I've got some bad news too. That developer's withdrawn his offer. He's had a word with someone at the council and he doesn't think he'll get planning permission to convert into flats. Apparently, they're worried that too many hotels in the road have already been converted. Look, I don't really want to talk about it on the phone. Can I come round later?'

'Of course.'

★ ★ ★

When I got back, Mike was sitting in his car on the forecourt.

'Sorry,' I said. 'I was chatting to Gail and didn't realise the time.'

'Don't worry.' He smiled as he got out. 'Did you see Caroline?'

'Tomorrow.'

'Great. I, er, got a little something for the baby.' He gestured to his car and I saw my ted's twin, blue-ribboned, sitting on the back seat.

'Perfect,' I said, resolving to hide my ted. Otherwise Robbie wouldn't be the only one accusing his parents of not communicating.

We sat in the kitchen and Mike said, 'Look, say if you think this is a mad idea, but maybe we could carry on for another season. We're a good team, you and me. Then we could put in for planning permission to convert this place into flats ourselves. If we don't get it we could appeal. We'd . . . well, we'd make a lot more money.'

I looked into his eyes and I thought of us working together again and all that it would lead to, and I thought about the sea outside our window and taking Caroline and our grandchild to our beautiful beach. Then, more irrationally, I thought how pleased George and Mabel, who'd spent too many happy holidays with us, would be if they could come here on their golden wedding anniversary.

'It's worth thinking about,' I said slowly, and I realised that Robbie had been right. Our crazy, misguided son had been right all along. We'd be mad to chuck away the last nineteen years for want of a bit of communication.

'The other thing,' Mike said, his face hesitant, 'is that I'd like to come to the hospital with you tomorrow, if that's OK?'

And I just looked at him and smiled.

★　★　★

In the morning, Mike and I went together to the maternity unit and were directed by a Japanese nurse to Caroline's room.

She was sitting in bed, a tiny, white-wrapped bundle in her arms. She didn't see us straight away. She was murmuring something to her newborn daughter, her head bent so that her dark hair half hid her face.

As we got closer I could feel my throat aching. It was all I could do not to burst into tears. Mike had taken my hand, I realised, and was holding it very tightly.

'Hi, Caroline,' I said gently. 'How are you both?'

She looked up and her face broke into a smile. 'I'm amazing,' she said simply. 'Tired, but amazing.' She glanced at Mike and he let go of my hand and stepped forward.

'I hope you didn't mind me coming along?'

'You're my father, aren't you?' Her eyes were wide and dark. Mike just nodded slowly and I knew he was having as much difficulty as I was with words. Then Caroline broke the spell. Turning back to the baby in her arms, she said, 'Well, now, Alison junior, here are some more grandparents for you to meet. I'm calling her Alison after my mum,' she added, looking at me, her eyes uncertain. 'I mean, she'll always be my mum, won't she?'

'Of course she will, love,' I said.

Then she smiled again and said, 'Thanks — for understanding. But that doesn't mean I don't want us to stay in touch. I mean, if you want to, that is?'

'We'd like that very much,' I murmured.

'Would you both like to hold her?' Caroline asked shyly and Mike and I looked at each other and said simultaneously, 'After you, love.'

And I thought that we might have a long way to go, but for once we'd got this communication business absolutely spot on.

THE END

We do hope that you have enjoyed reading this large print book.

Did you know that all of our titles are available for purchase?

We publish a wide range of high quality large print books including:
Romances, Mysteries, Classics
General Fiction
Non Fiction and Westerns

Special interest titles available in large print are:
The Little Oxford Dictionary
Music Book, Song Book
Hymn Book, Service Book

Also available from us courtesy of Oxford University Press:
Young Readers' Dictionary
(large print edition)
Young Readers' Thesaurus
(large print edition)

For further information or a free brochure, please contact us at:
Ulverscroft Large Print Books Ltd.,
The Green, Bradgate Road, Anstey,
Leicester, LE7 7FU, England.
Tel: (00 44) **0116 236 4325**
Fax: (00 44) **0116 234 0205**

HEARTS IN EXILE

Catriona McCuaig

Two teachers are evacuated from Coventry to the Welsh countryside, where they struggle with wartime hardship as they help their pupils adjust to a different way of life. Will love follow them there? Vivacious Tansy sees marriage as a way to escape her impoverished background, while shy Dinah just wants to find someone to love. She falls for handsome Emlyn, but the young Welshman is equally reserved. How will they ever get together?

A PAIR OF SKY-BLUE EYES

Jasmina Svenne

After two years of nursing the casualties of the Great War, Clara Allingham thinks she is immune to love. But something about the withdrawn Captain William Morton touches her and makes her determined to heal his psychological scars, as well as his physical wounds. However, as the war grinds on, both Clara and William have to choose whether to lock up their hearts and keep themselves safe — or to risk everything for love.

DREAM OF DANGER

Anne Hewland

Recently widowed, following a marriage of convenience, Madeleine Corning grieves for the loss of her baby son. She's grateful for the protection of her late husband's cousin, Cornelius, although her loyal servant Ellen believes he's not trustworthy — and that her child still lives. Should Madeleine turn to stranger William Franklyn for help — but why has he been watching her house? And he is not the only one, it seems. She must undergo danger and treachery to unravel the truth.